W9-BIJ-333

this book belongs to

_____

Visit Little Lucy & Friends™ at
www.littlelucyandfriends.com
and www.playhousepublishing.com.

Library of Congress Cataloging-in-Publication Data

Kapper, R. Jon.
Bow Wow Blast Off / author, R. Jon Kapper ; creator, Deborah D'Andrea;
clay illustrator, Jon Ottinger; dog photographer, Rick Zaidan. - 1st ed.   p. cm.

Summary: Lucy, Petie, and Dizzy are trapped inside a space capsule on a
field trip to the Space Dog Museum with Miss Bowser's class.
ISBN 1-57151-702-2 (Hardcover) -- ISBN 1-57151-707-3 (Paperback)
[1. Dogs--Fiction. 2. School field trips--Fiction.
3. Museums--Fiction.] I. D'Andrea, Deborah. II. Ottinger, Jon, ill. III.
Zaidan, Rick, ill. IV. Title.
PZ7.K12955 Bo 2001
[E]--dc21
2001002937

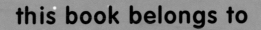

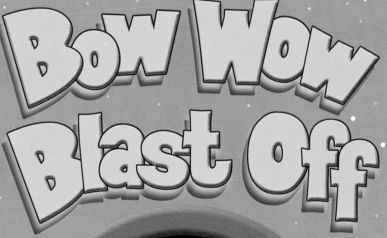

Bow Wow Blast Off

LITTLE Lucy & FRIENDS

Creator: Deborah D'Andrea, Ed.S.
Author: R. Jon Kapper
Clay Illustrator: Jon Ottinger
Dog Photographer: Rick Zaidan
Designer: Erik Powers
Design Assistant: Lynne Schwaner

PLAYHOUSE PUBLISHING

Akron, Ohio

Miss Bowser's class yapped excitedly as they entered the Space Dog Museum on their annual field trip.

They looked up in amazement at the flickering stars and colorful planets that filled the Planetarium. "Miss Bowser, what is that bright star over there?" Little Lucy asked.

"That is Sirius, the brightest star in the night sky," said Miss Bowser. "It is also known as Dog Star."

"Where is Dog Star's tail?" Lucy whispered to Petie.

"I guess he doesn't have one," Petie answered as they turned to follow the others to the space capsule exhibit.

The class stopped to admire the large space capsule in the center of the exhibit hall. Petie and Dizzy followed Lucy up the steps and through the open hatch to have a look inside.

Spike jumped up and grabbed onto the capsule's rocket booster. "Hey, look at me. I'm flying!" he squealed.

"You come down from there, Spike," scolded Miss Bowser.

Spike swung left, then right and finally, off of the rocket booster. All this swinging caused the capsule to tilt and suddenly, the hatch began to close.

Verne dropped his bag of Meteorite Nuggets and jumped to catch the swinging hatch.

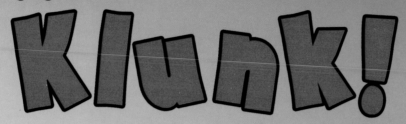

The hatch knocked Verne on the head and latched shut.

"Hhheeelllppp!!!" cried Dizzy from inside the capsule.

Spike tried the handle on the hatch but it would not open.

"Shake a leg, you two," barked Miss Bowser to Verne and Spike. "We need to find someone who can help us rescue Lucy, Petie and Dizzy!"

Inside the capsule, Lucy's imagination was taking flight. "I have an idea," she announced. "Let's make believe we are Astrodogs going on a mission into space."

"I think I'm going to faint!" panted Dizzy.

"Geeze fleas! There's Dog Star," Petie yelped.

"Hey, let's take him his missing tail as part of our mission," suggested Lucy.

"Great idea," declared Petie. "We'd better put on our space suits and get ready to blast off!"

Miss Bowser burst into the Museum Gift Shop. "Come quick," she begged.

"Now don't get your tail all tied in knots, Ma'am," responded Jaws, the museum's watchdog. "What seems to be the problem?"

"Lucy, Petie and Dizzy are locked inside one of the space capsules," explained Miss Bowser.

"Well, what are we just standing around here for?" asked Jaws, as he stuffed a doughnut into his mouth. "Let's go!"

It was all systems go inside the space capsule. "Petie, ignite the fire rockets," ordered Lucy.

Petie pushed a green button on the control panel and the capsule began to move.

"Dog Star, here we come!" shouted Lucy.

The rescue team arrived on the scene to find the capsule rocking back and forth. Spike raced to the capsule and took a look inside.

Petie noticed someone peering through the hatch window. "Houston, we have a problem," he announced. "A Martian is trying to enter the space capsule."

"Let's shake him loose," barked Lucy. She pulled the blue lever. The capsule began to spin around and around.

Yeehaw!

Spike howled, holding onto the capsule as it spun wildly.

Jaws stepped toward the capsule and grabbed at Spike as he swung by him. "Doggone it. If I could only lay my paws on him," he huffed.

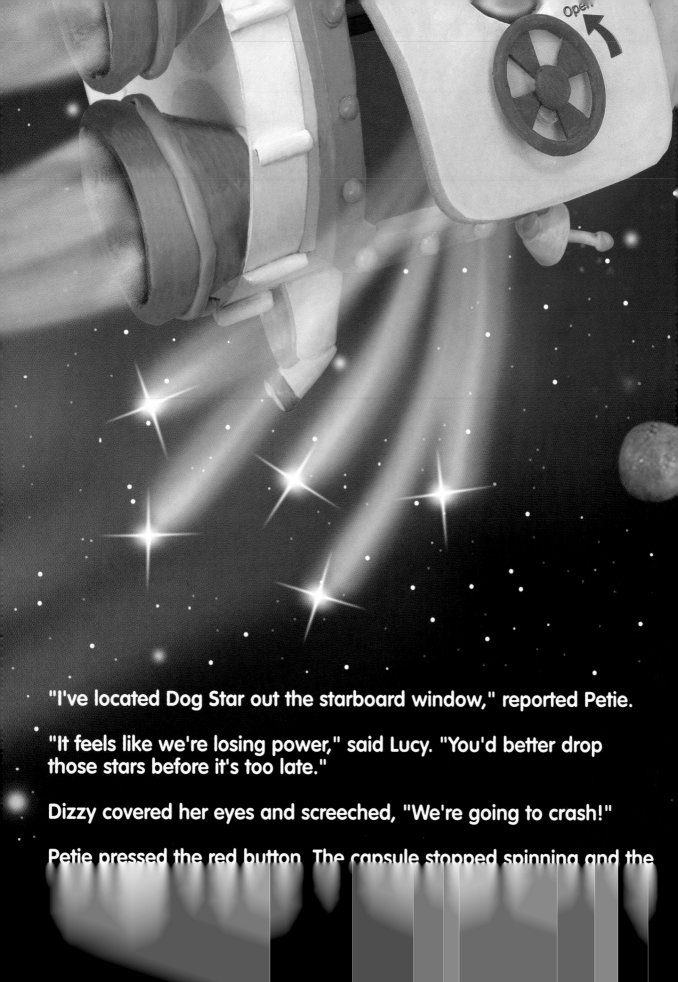

"I've located Dog Star out the starboard window," reported Petie.

"It feels like we're losing power," said Lucy. "You'd better drop those stars before it's too late."

Dizzy covered her eyes and screeched, "We're going to crash!"

Petie pressed the red button. The capsule stopped spinning and the

Lucy, Petie and Dizzy climbed out of the capsule.

"Well, you three certainly had an exciting adventure," sighed a relieved Miss Bowser.

"It was a small step for a dog but a giant leap for dogkind!" exclaimed Lucy as the class headed towards the museum exit.

At bedtime, Lucy stared out of her window at the night sky. She could see the glowing moon and Dog Star shining brightly.

Suddenly, something moved across the sky. Lucy looked at Dog Star again and for an instant she thought she saw the tail wagging.

Lucy smiled. "Good night, Dog Star. Sweet dreams," she whispered, and closed her eyes.

This book is dedicated to Joe, Noelle, and David
my light and joy.—DBD

This book is dedicated to my two childhood dogs: Prince,
who was poisoned by the neighbor, and Ginger, who, despite
being hit twice by automobiles, lived a long and full life.—RJK

Many thanks to the dog breeders and dogs
who helped make the book characters come to life:

Randy and Terry Stackhouse of Casa de Chihuahua, owners of Cordoba (Spike)
Mary Jo Baranowski of Primrose Poodles, owner of Mi Mi (Dizzy)
Mary Ann Holland, owner of Shakespeare (Petie)
Cathy Gillmore, owner of Lady (Miss Bowser)
Pamela Salomone of Double D's Kennels, owner of Cashmere (Jaws)
and of course, my two dogs,
Lucy and Rico (Verne).

Special thanks to:

Jackie Wolf our editor who now knows more
about Astrodogs than she ever thought possible.

Kaycee Hoffman for her graphic design assistance.

Ann Longenecker, our talented costume seamstress.

ACTIVITY: MAKE YOUR OWN DOG STAR

Join Little Lucy and her fellow Astrodogs by taking a trip to the stars yourself. Just follow the directions below to create your own Dog Star. Then buckle in and blast off!

And remember, when you're flying around up there, to say hello to Dog Star and leave a few stars behind for his tail.

WHAT YOU NEED:
★ Sharpened pencil or something to poke holes through paper
★ A flashlight

WHAT TO DO:
With the assistance of a parent, guardian or much older sibling:

1. Remove the page on the right from the book.

2. Use the pattern of circles as a guide. Poke holes through the page at each dot. Make sure the holes are wide enough to allow light to pass through. ✕ ➞ ●

3. Turn off the lights.

4. Hold the punched activity page in one hand and hold a flashlight in the other hand underneath the page.

5. The light will shine through the holes and Dog Star will be visible on your ceiling.

OTHER FUN ACTIVITIES

★ Miss Bowser's homework assignment is for you to draw your own picture of Dog Star. If you want, you can include the Astrodogs and their space capsule too.

★ Now wouldn't it be fun to gather around with friends and create your own story about other missions the Astrodogs take into outer space? Maybe they even go to Mars in search of buried dog bones.

★ Once the sun sets, Little Lucy and her pals love to roll around on the cool grass and gaze at the stars. Why not join them? If you want to be like Verne, you might even try howling at the moon.